GW00871549

Captain ...... and the Mermaid

William Mayne found it was easier to
write books than do his schoolwork,
and had his first one published in 1953.
By the millennium he will have had
about a hundred in print, but he still
thinks he works very slowly and spends
whole days looking out of the window
not doing the gardening and pretending
he is thinking. When it is dark he gets
out the ink and writes words down
until they make sense. He thinks you
don't get much done if you are busy.

Text Copyright © 1999 William Mayne
Illustrations Copyright © 1999 William Geldart

First published in hardback in Great Britain in 1999
by Hodder Children's Books

This paperback edition published in 1999
by Hodder Children's Books

The right of William Mayne and William Geldart to be identified as the Author and Illustrator
of the Work has been asserted by them in accordance with the Copyright, Designs
and Patents Act 1988.

10 9 8 7 6 5 4 3 2 1

All rights reserved. No part of this publication may be reproduced, stored in a retrieval system,
or transmitted, in any form or by any means, without the prior written permission of the
publisher, nor be otherwise circulated in any form of binding or cover other than that in which
it is published and without a similar condition being imposed on the subsequent purchaser.

All characters in this publication are fictitious and any resemblance to real persons, living
or dead, is purely coincidental.

A Catalogue record for this book is available from the British Library

ISBN 0 340 73677 1

Printed and bound in Great Britain by
Clays Ltd, St Ives plc

Hodder Children's Books
A division of Hodder Headline
338 Euston Road
London NW1 3BH

Captain Ming
and the Mermaid

William Mayne

Illustrated by William Geldart

Hodder
Children's
Books

a division of Hodder Headline

For Rosie Dinsdale

ONE

Lucy did not get many letters. The people she knew lived close by, and a lot of them could not write yet because they were too young.

"Aren't you going to open it?" Mum asked.

"I don't know who wrote it," said Lucy. "I've seen the writing at school, but no one there writes to me."

She poured milk on cereal and began to eat it.

"Is it my birthday?" she asked Mum. "Did I invite myself? Do I want to go to her party?" Could the snowman she had just built in the garden have written? He did not look clever, and one eye had fallen out. Lucy took her time, and a piece of toast.

"The stamp is from Scotland," she said. "It's got a thistle on it. You can get stamps anywhere. There was no need to go to . . ." But then she knew who the letter was from. "Morag," she said. "Her writing. We met her last summer on the school trip on the puffer. It's her uncle's steamer, and she goes across the loch on it to school. She writes to our school about what happens in Scotland."

"Open it," said Mum. "See what it says."

"I won't even take it to school," said Lucy, working things out. "Morag will have written to everyone, even awful people like Craig."

Lucy kept things for ever, first in her bag of findings, then clean and neat in boxes and cupboards, and knew where they all were, things she had found and no one else had seen, in hedges or under stones, or forgotten at the back of shops.

Last year, at the Scottish loch, she had found part of the silvery bridle of Kelpie, a magical water-horse, and mended it with a strand of snakeskin already in her findings bag. She had tried to put it on Kelpie again, with no luck until Craig helped her. Craig had understood Kelpie, and calmed and managed him, and between them they had put the bridle on.

Otherwise Craig was too sudden, too rough, too loud, too unkind, always got his own way, bang, crash, and disregarded everybody else.

"I'll put it away," said Lucy, "and

share someone else's." But, as soon as she had said it she slit the envelope open and pulled the letter out. She checked the signature, which read, "Morag" and underneath, "Morag MacAlister" in neat print.

"Dear Lucy," the letter said, "It is a long time since I wrote to the school. Please tell them Thank you for their letters. This one is just for you."

"It's for me," said Lucy. "Only for me."

"What does it say?" asked Mum.

"That's all, so far," said Lucy. She read more.

"We have had a wee bit of trouble with the puffer," Morag went on. "I had to stay with Granny MacAlister the other side of the loch for several weeks during the winter, or I would not have got to my lessons. My uncle, Captain Ming, has set things right for now, but at Easter he is to take it down the river to Glasgow.

My mother and I will go with him to
visit my Auntie while it is getting
repaired. It gets done every seven years.
I went when I was five, and slept on
board and had a grand time."

"She's going sailing," said Lucy. "If
I write I can tell her nothing, because
that's all I've done."

The letter went on, "My mother and
I thought you might like to come with us,

because you were so good at helping
Kelpie last year. I do not believe at all in
Kelpie and things like that, but it will be
helpful to have someone with us who
does."

"Believe?" said Lucy. "I don't have
to believe in Kelpie. I saw him and
touched him. It's Craig I would
unbelieve in if I could."

"Is Craig invited as well?" said Mum.

"No," said Lucy, "of course not."

"Glasgow," the letter went on, "is a
fine town, and my cousins are great fun.
The eldest one is eleven, just halfway
between you and me. I hope you can
come with us. I will meet you at the end
of the railway on the far lochside where
the puffer waits for the train. We shall be
at the farm for a few days, and then set
off down the river."

"Railway?" said Lucy. "I'm going on
the train as well," she told Mum. "Just me."

"Do you want to go?" said Mum. "You weren't sure about the school trip, but you were very young then."

"I want to go," said Lucy. "I'll believe in Kelpie day and night."

"'And things like that,' it says," said Mum.

"All those things," said Lucy.

"I've had a letter from Mrs MacAlister too," said Mum. "If you'd like to go, write back and say so."

"I'll pack straight away," said Lucy. "Where can I get an English stamp with flowers on it? Where will I get on the train?"

"Mrs MacAlister has invited me to come across to the farm with you for a night to settle you in," said Mum. "If that's all right with you, write back as soon as you like, but don't pack for several weeks, because Easter is a long way off."

Lucy decided not to speak about the letter at school, in case Craig told her alarming things about Scotland. But you can't prevent mums talking, and people at school heard about it.

Elspbeth said, "It'll be nice if you aren't homesick." She had been homesick on the school trip.

Craig said, "That's rubbish, Scotland." He managed to knock Lucy's wet painting off the table and tread on it. "I'm off to Ashton in the holiday. I think it's in Cornwall."

Lucy wrote back to Morag, accepting the invitation, and promising to believe in Kelpie as much as necessary.

Morag wrote back. "Kelpie is one thing," she said. "There are other things people believe in. It can be a help to have someone to sort things out."

"Sort things out?" said Mum. "What does she mean?"

"I'll find something that will help," said Lucy. "I'll keep looking." She carried the findings bag with her always. Now there was nothing to put in it, because bright hazel catkins, or snowdrops pushing through the frost, would die if she gathered them. And no one finds a silver snakeskin twice in a lifetime.

One morning her snowman had sunk into his boots. Two matching stones with curly hollow places lay on the grass, a glitter of gold and a thawed tear in each. They had been his eyes. The curly thing that made the hollows was an ammonite. It lived in a drawer upstairs, looking like solid gold. Lucy got it at the seaside last summer, from a boy who split rocks open to find fossils.

She had a seaside comb from that
holiday, to use every day. She taped
the ammonite in its stony case, and put
it in her bag.

The snowman melted quite away.
Easter came near.

TWO

Lucy thought it would be best to
start the journey to Scotland as
soon as she woke up and knew
this was the day. Her backpack in the
corner of the room proved it. Without
moving, she closed her eyes again.

I'm turning my head off, she
thought. The rest of me is still asleep.
Craig and Elspbeth and everyone will
wake up and go to school. I am taking
today and tomorrow off to travel on a

steamer. I am not at home. I am lying in my bed on the puffer. When I get up I shall be there without having to wait. I can smell the smoke.

Smoke would climb from the funnel and blow away along the loch, but some of it would come down to put black marks on passengers' noses and sneezes inside.

The water-horse was galloping outside, Kelpie come to see the puffer, come to look at the wheels on either side, to see his friends.

"Are you getting up?" asked Kelpie, leaning over the side. It was Mum in the doorway. The smoke from the funnel was scorched breakfast toast downstairs.

"I was there already," said Lucy.

Later on she watched the clock. It was clearly ill, but each time she knew it had stopped and they must leave at once, it twitched its hands in a sickly way.

"I don't believe it," she said, quite often.

Then they were at the station, and a train was stopping and standing still and its doors breathing open.

"In here," said Mum. "We reserved our places."

Halfway through a train sandwich there was a notice about the fields outside being Scotland. "We are nearly there," said Lucy, dribbling crumbs.

"Chew slowly," said Mum. "There's an hour or two yet. About the time the others come out of school we shall be there."

Lucy thought a river outside might be the one they would travel on, under the bridges, through the fields, among the woods.

Later on water lay alongside the train, a small sea or a big loch, blue like a map. Maps have names written in a neat curve, but there was nothing here, unless a bird swinging overhead could read something.

"What's that out on the lake?" said Mum.

"Loch," said Lucy.

There was smoke out on the water, a smudge being spread by the wind, a dirty thumb marking the map. Under the smoke there was a line along the water, and a roundness at the middle of it.

"The puffer," said Lucy. "That's the puffer. That's the smoke, and that's the paddle wheel."

"I see you ken your way aboot," said the other passenger. "That'll be Captain Ming on his way to meet this very train."

"I ken that," said Lucy, saying the right thing in Scotland. "We're going on it."

The puffer out on the water seemed not to be moving. If it breaks down, Lucy thought, then Kelpie pushes it to the landing stage. Morag had written to the school and told them that last year. But the train was going slower among houses. People were getting their luggage and moving towards the doors.

Morag was waiting on the landing stage, which was part of the railway platform. She was looking very tidy in her school clothes.

Lucy took her first breath of true Scottish air.

"I have been at the Academy all day," said Morag. "So it was nae trouble to meet you. How do you do? Have you had a good journey? Now here's the puffer tying up, and letting us on board."

The puffer was very close now, and a man was waiting to throw it a rope. The puffer pushed at the landing stage and made it creak. When ropes were hitched it stopped moving. Passengers got off for the train, for the town, or their cars.

Lucy was on board first, looking for her dream bedroom. There was a ladies' cabin, and animals at the front of the boat, but no pink curtains.

Mum and Morag looked at the far side of the loch.

"The white house up the hill," Morag was saying, "is the farm. The house by the loch shore is the hostel."

"I will show you my room there," said Lucy. "And where Elspbeth was homesick."

Out on the loch something stirred the water.

"A fish," said Morag. "That's all."

"It might be Kelpie," said Lucy. "Look hard."

The puffer coughed and spluttered. The steam whistle cleared its throat, and shouted. Drops of warm grey water splashed on Mum.

The whistle came back again from the far side of the loch. "Kelpie does that," Lucy said. "I ken."

"An echo," said Morag. "Just the echo."

Kelpie, if it was he, did not call again.

THREE

M ost passengers got off at the far side of the loch. "It's a school party at the hostel," said Morag. "We'll let them get clear. Will you hold my bag? I'm away to help the shepherds with the lambs."

At the front of the puffer the rail had been lifted and a floor of planks laid over the gap. Shepherds were taking ewes and lambs out of the stock pen. The idea was new to the lambs, but the mothers had been on the puffer before. Morag had also done this before, and she knew the shepherds and the dogs, who waved their tails when they saw her.

"Here a week early, for-by," said one shepherd.

"Will you all gae wi'the captain?" asked another.

"Some one has to be with him," said Morag. "Ye ken his problem."

The shepherds laughed, and waved to the puffer. The captain waved back from the high part.

"She probably knows the sheep too," said Mum. "Do you, Morag?"

"Some of them," said Morag, "might know me. They're over early, because the puffer is away next week, and the sheep have to be on the muirs. Moors is the English word. Before the puffer they came miles round the head of the loch, or over in a rowing boat."

The steamer shouted with its whistle. The puffer set off on the next leg of its voyage round the loch.

The school party trudged to the hostel. The dogs walked the sheep and the shepherds off.

There was a deserted landing stage, a puff of smoke from the steamer on the water, and the beginning of a lane, empty now that the sheep had gone.

"This is very far away," said Mum.

"That is why we need the puffer," said Morag. "When it broke down in winter with a damaged paddle I had to stay in the town, because of the blocked lanes between here and town, round the head of the loch."

They began walking up the lane. They had not far to go before a tractor and trailer met them.

"It's your taxi," said Morag. "It is my Dad."

"Alexander MacAlister," he said. "Sandy."

"Ruth," said Mum.

"And this the wee lass that sorted things oot?" said Sandy. "You'll not count as strangers here."

"I ken," said Lucy.

They rode up to the farm in the trailer.

"Oh my," said Mum, in the long kitchen with its three tables, and the huge fireplace blazing in the shadows. "I'd better go, or I'll settle in for ever."

"We wouldna move away," said Morag's mother. "Just the odd trip to Glasgow, and we're happy here year in and year out."

Lucy had a cupboard bed in Morag's room, with her own little window overlooking the loch in the distance. "I wouldn't bother with Glasgow," she said. "I'd always be thinking of coming back here."

Later on Morag took milk down to the hostel. Mum and Lucy went with her. Lucy had it in mind to show Mum her room from last year. But at the hostel all the children were unknown, and the wrong size.

Lucy did not want to go in, because the rooms would be strangers' rooms, with nothing she wanted to remember for herself, or Mum to see.

Mum stayed two nights at the farm, and then she was going up the gangway of the puffer alone, too early in the day for walkers or the hostel children.

Lucy was alone as well, the puffer was going away, Mum was hardly to be seen, and the tractor and trailer were wanted at the farm.

"Will you be all right?" asked Morag, because the end of Lucy's nose had got runny by itself, her eyes had got hot, and her tummy felt like a lost lamb. Lucy knew Sandy could telephone the station and get Mum to come back and take her home the next day. But she just asked for a hanky.

There was only the tractor's one. Lucy dabbed at a sniffle, and let the tractor have the oily rag back. Then she had no time for anything else, because the farm sheep had to be walked up to their summer grazing on the farm's own muirs.

"At the top," said Morag, "it's heather right to the sea. You can see it, and beyond."

They walked to the top along a drove road, with Morag occasionally driving the tractor. The sheep walked all the way. Everybody waited for the lambs.

The flock went into a huge brown field, where the heather was still sleepy. Sandy took Lucy and Morag higher up to see over the top. The wind blew in their faces so that Lucy's nose ran again. So did Morag's. They saw the far-away sea.

"Clouds on it," said Lucy.

"Islands," said Sandy. "Eanster and Faransay, and Clowder. They take sheep there from the coast."

When they came down the sheep were homesick and wanting to come out of the gateway again.

"In three months or so it will take the day and more to gather them together," said Sandy.

"It will be a job for ponies," said Morag.

"I will come back for it," said Lucy. She bit her tongue as the tractor bounced, and this time a tear ran across her cheek. It was only her tongue hurting.

The next day was Sunday, and Sandy read the Bible to them at breakfast. They went to church, and there were sheepdogs under the seats.

They had a quiet day with a big meal in the middle. In the afternoon Lucy helped Morag put together things for the journey. Instead of taking Morag across to the Academy in the morning the puffer would collect her, her mother, and Lucy, and set off straight down the loch.

"Then into the river," said Morag. "It's a wild place, and no roads near, and we have to get to the end of it at the right time to cross the bar."

Mrs MacAlister explained that the bar was a shallow place where the river joined the firth, and the water beyond had to lift with the tide, or the puffer would stick and maybe be wrecked.

"And that's me packed," said Morag, tying a last knot, and getting up to answer the telephone. "What are people doing telephoning on the Sabbath?"

Her mother came to the telephone. "Oh dear," she was saying at once. "I will come away on the puffer tomorrow. Captain Ming will take me back."

She put the telephone down.

"Granny MacAlister," she said. Lucy had heard of Granny MacAlister, who was bedfast.

"Fallen from her bed and broken her leg," said Mrs MacAlister. "We shall not be going with my brother to Glasgow tomorrow. He will have to go on his own and we must stay behind to look after her."

FOUR

Morag's mother said, "It is the worst time for it. With the puffer at Glasgow I shall have to stay in town instead of ferrying over in the day to get my own work done between times."

She got out a loaf of bread. "But there is nothing to be done until the morn," she went on, snicking off a slice of farm butter and spreading it on the loaf. "Then we'll have to see."

Lucy saw and heard what she had come for vanishing, if no one was to go on the puffer. Mrs MacAlister looked at her, quick and thoughtful. A smile meant, "Don't worry about us." It also meant, "What shall we do with you? This is no time for visitors."

They will put me on the train, Lucy thought. But I would like to stay, if I am not in the way.

Sandy came in, and saw the tea not quite ready, and knew that something was wrong.

"There is no cause to worry," said Mrs MacAlister. "But your mother has broken her leg by falling from her bed."

"I have heard of the like with very old folk," said Sandy. "Shall I take you round the head of the loch and see her and you stay with her?"

"The puffer tomorrow morning will be soon enough," said Mrs MacAlister.

"Tonight she will be under anaesthetic, so there is nothing to do, and no puffer this whole week to bring me across the loch. I shall not be on it, wherever it is."

"No," said Sandy, slowly, looking at Morag, and at Lucy. "We will be thinking what to do."

The kettle boiled. Mrs MacAlister brought out a Sunday pie from the warming oven, and tea began. Lucy could not eat much, with the promise of tomorrow's finest journey taken away from her, even though the pie was the best one she had ever had on her plate. The pie became misty. The gravy wrinkled from a tear that landed on it.

"Now, what is the matter?" asked Mrs MacAlister.

I mustn't bother her, thought Lucy.

"I bit my tongue," she said, with a wobbly voice.

"Morag," said Sandy, "there is a new calf in the fold, and you would like to show it to Lucy, and the pair of you have your tea in a bit. I will talk with your mother while I have mine."

"That will be fine," said Morag. She said to Lucy, "They will be wanting to talk medical details." She put an arm round Lucy, and led her out into the sunshine. "Come and see him," she said.

He was a Highland calf. His legs were made of wobbling joints, his tail stuck out instead of hanging, and he was wet round the ears. His mother licked him dry, which made him wet again. He did not know what anything was except his mother.

"We'll sit on the straw outside," said Morag at the fold door. "They're a wild breed. When he grows up he will have great wide horns, and be a prize beast you would not want to meet on the muir."

He sucked their fingers, and went for milk to his mother. She mooed happily and shuffled her feet. The calf tripped over the straw and dribbled.

"Have I to go home?" Lucy asked.

"I don't know," said Morag. "There will be so much to do, and we'll do one of them now." She had heard the voices of children at the hostel. "They're back, and they will be wanting their milk."

That worked out very well, at exactly the right time. Morag filled the can and Lucy put the top on.

They were crossing to the gate with it when Sandy called for Morag to come in for a minute.

"I'm away with milk for the hostel," Morag said.

"I'll do it," said Lucy. "By myself. I know how."

"Come straight back," said Morag. Lucy went alone, with the milk keeping step in the can.

"Thank you," said the teacher at the kitchen door. "Tell your mother I'll be up tomorrow to pay."

"Yes," said Lucy, taking an empty can from him (not very clean), walking out of the gate and up the hill, the can singing to itself when the lid moved.

There was a stone by the path. Lucy sat on it and looked at the loch, pretended she was lost, and had her cry.

I'm sorry for Granny MacAlister, she thought, and I hope it doesn't hurt her, but I'm crying for me. One more ride on the puffer in the morning, and they don't want me any more. She found herself, and hurried back to the farm.

She put the milk can on the stone bench, and went in. Mrs MacAlister was telephoning. Morag put a finger to her lips. "Tea?" she whispered. She brought out the pie, and made tea in a small pot. Mrs MacAlister talked quietly at the far end of the long room.

"Whatever time we have," said Morag, "we'll make it a nice one and be glad of what we have."

"Yes," said Lucy, and burnt her tongue.

When Mrs MacAlister called her to the telephone she was breathing over the hot pie with her mouth open, unable to speak.

"It's your mother," said Mrs MacAlister.

Lucy made breathing and yelping noises, with a hand politely over her mouth. Morag took the telephone to explain. Lucy swallowed food much too hot.

"I hear it's good weather," said Mum, at last. "You will be wanting that."

"No," said Lucy, bravely, feeling herself flutter with disappointment. "Are you coming to get me?"

"No," said Mum. "Why? Mrs MacAlister said you were looking forward to the voyage. Aren't you?"

"We can't go," said Lucy. "Nobody can go."

"Mrs MacAlister said you girls would go alone," said Mum. "The Captain is her brother."

"No," said Lucy. Mum did not make sense. "Yes."

"Her sister will ring when you land," said Mum. "Someone has to go with him, because of his problem."

"Problem?" said Lucy.

"Yes," said Mum. "The mermaid."

FIVE

When Mum said, "The mermaid," Lucy had no idea how to answer. She didn't know all the telephone rules.

All she could do was stretch out her telephoning hand, give the black thing to Mrs MacAlister, and go back to Morag, who didn't look as if she had had strange things said to her.

Morag smiled, then popped in another piece of pastry, saying at the same time, "So was that all right, then?"

"The telephone went wrong," said Lucy. But the time had not been wasted, because the pie was no longer too hot. She could fill her mouth with that, not with words that did not explain anything.

Mrs MacAlister put down the telephone. Sandy came in again, in the middle of farm work, but wanting to know what was going on.

"What was the end of it?" he asked. "What did the bairn's mother think of the job?"

"She thought well enough of it," said Mrs MacAlister. "What does the bairn think?"

"She doesn't know," said Morag. "Did you not listen, Lucy? To your mother?"

"I didn't know what the telephone was saying," Lucy told her. "It was only my Mum. Was it awful?"

"It's this," said Mrs MacAlister. "I can't go on the steamer to Glasgow. Someone sensible has to go, like Morag, and you will go with Morag. Captain Ming will look after you, and you will look after him."

That made sense, if you didn't think your Mum had talked about mermaids. But, thought Lucy, even if they tease me for being wrong, I'll say what mistake the telephone made, and . . .

"I thought Mum said mermaid," she told them, and went on with another lump of pie. Now that it was not too hot it was very good. If the telephone had made the mistake no one would blame Lucy.

"He's had the problem many years," said Mrs MacAlister, not hearing

43

any mistakes. "Since he was just a young lad. We thought he had forgotten her, when he married Alison and had his own bairns. But when he was widowed, the next time he went down the river and out to sea, why, the mermaid was there again. Seven years after that, but before I was married, I went to keep him from her. The last time, seven years ago, Morag and I went with him. So it's still a problem."

"I can manage it," said Morag. "We can."

"I would like to see a mermaid," said Lucy. She did not consider there was a problem for Captain Ming in seeing one. A cat may look at a king, after all.

"But," said Sandy, "it's not *seeing* her. Did no one say? He's fallen in love with her. The daft loon, if he is my own brother-in-law."

"And she is in love with him," said Mrs MacAlister. "Last time, on the trial trip round the islands, to see that everything was mended and fitted right, she followed us back and away up the firth."

"From Eanster, and Faransay," said Sandy. "We think she lives near little Clowder. She follows steamers, and if they aren't the puffer she goes back home. And if it is the puffer she stays with it."

"And one day," said Mrs MacAlister, "if Captain Ming, isn't kept an eye on, he will stay with her."

"But he won't be happy marrying a mermaid," said Morag. "So we have to stop him seeing her, and her from seeing him."

Lucy put her last piece of pie in. Now she did not have to speak. But she understood. It was quite clear and reasonable to her. Mum might not have understood enough, and had not been able to explain.

"I managed about Kelpie," she said, with a great gulp of pie out of the way, "I can manage about this." Something would turn up, like a snakeskin, smooth and binding.

"Kelpie is not real," said Morag. "I don't believe in it."

"Him," said Lucy.

"I do believe in the mermaid," said Morag, "even if she doesn't exist either."

"Captain Ming and the puffer will come over at seven for me and take me across," said Mrs MacAlister, "and then set off to Glasgow with you."

Before seven the next morning Lucy carried her backpack to the landing stage, with Morag and Mrs MacAlister. Morag had her own bag, and a can of milk for the puffer, to use on the voyage.

Mrs MacAlister had the suitcase she had got ready for Glasgow. Three passengers boarded the puffer.

The other side of the loch the puffer tied up. A man played the bagpipes on the landing stage, and a crowd listened round him. One passenger got off. Mrs MacAlister kissed Morag, gave Lucy a little shoulder-hug, and went down the gangway with her suitcase.

As soon as she had gone, the crowd of people marched on board, the bagpiper playing amongst them, and filled all the deck.

"Away up to the bridge, Lucy," said Morag. "There is more room up there, and we shan't spill the milk."

The puffer left the stage and set off down the loch, blowing its own whistle so that the echoes came back over the water. After the whistle nothing could be

heard above the piper, screaming up
and down the deck. When he stopped
to drink, a train sounded its hooter and
church bells rang. People on the landing
stage began to shout and cheer, and car
horns yelled.

"I thought it would be a quiet
voyage," said Lucy, her hands to her
ears. What will Kelpie make of it? she
wondered, privately.

"Aye, noisy," Morag shouted. "It's an occasion. I forgot they did this. It willna be for very long."

Land noises faded away. Only the piper walked the deck below, swinging his kilt and skirling the sound of the pipes across the loch. But now they were on the water the sound leaked away better.

SIX

The puffer leaned to one side and changed direction. Captain Ming sounded his whistle twice, to show that the puffer was changing course. "We're off down the water," he said, "and I want no fisherman to be in our path and not see us. The paddles can grind a man up awfu' badly. Can ye swim?"

"Fifty metres," said Lucy, showing him the badge from the findings bag, where it lived with snowman's eyes and their golden ammonite.

"If ye tumble o'erboard," said Captain Ming, handing the badge back, "take this with ye. If it works we'll fish ye oot."

Lucy remembered that last year a calf had jumped into the water, and been rescued by Kelpie. She was certain that if necessary Kelpie would rescue her, and there was nothing to worry about.

"But I shan't fall in," she told Morag. "Even if it's quite safe."

"It's drinking water," said Morag, "and it would drink you."

The piper's tunes were carried over the water on the wind. People brought out sandwiches and flasks of tea, and laughed at the way the tea slopped on the deck when their hands swayed.

"Noo, breakfast," said Captain Ming,

licking his lips. "Morag, ye ken what to do. Away below, tell Lachlan to brew the tea and stir the oatmeal, and fetch it back up here. I'm needing a bite to eat." Lucy licked her own lips, because they felt dry. She was not ready for breakfast. She wished it had not been mentioned. Her feet were not able to hold the deck as they should. One was light and the other heavy, making her tummy think about itself.

A puff of wind came round a corner of the bridge and pushed her about in a dizzy way. The piper missed a snatch of tune. The paddles caught a wave with a rumbling gurgle and swallowed it noisily. Grinding it up awfu' badly, thought Lucy, shivering.

"What ails ye?" said Captain Ming to her. "Ye're a sailor now. We're short-handed the day, so ye have work to do, lassie. Hold this wheel a minute, while I

shout to my engine man. Don't turn it, or we'll be off course. Just steer to that mountain, the hill with the black hut on it."

The wheel had spokes that stuck out all round. Captain Ming clamped Lucy's hands on two of them, and left her there alone to drive the puffer while he went down the steps to the engine.

Lucy felt the water trying to turn the wheel another way, and held on, first with one hand and then the other, to steer towards the black hut.

Before Captain Ming returned, Morag was with her. "Do you know how to do it?" she asked, putting down a cooking pot of something hot and steamy beside the milk-can from the farm.

"I'm going to the mountain," said Lucy. "Easy."

Now she had work to do, the wind

was not making her dizzy at all, and she felt like breakfast.

"Careful, then, and watch the porridge," said Morag, and went down again for more breakfast.

Lucy steered as hard as she could, but the black hut stayed far off. She felt she needed a badge, for steering more than fifty metres.

Captain Ming came back, wiping black and greasy hands, and smelling of burnt coal. "Ye do well for a starter," he said. "Look back and see how you did."

Lucy looked back at the wake the steamer had left on the loch. It was as straight as you could get without a ruler, she thought. Captain Ming told her to keep at it and get it right in a year or two.

Morag came back with more breakfast, and began to serve it out. Captain Ming took the wheel again, steering with one foot, a bowl of porridge in one hand, a big spoon in the other, swallowing stuff so hot that Lucy was having to blow on hers for a long time before daring to get it in her mouth.

She took the smallest spoon, sure she could not eat much. But she had porridge, bannock and bacon, and smoky tea, more than she would eat at home.

Morag took the empty bowls, plates, and mugs, down the step again. Captain Ming looked all round. He was preparing to get to land without any help, and there was no mermaid in sight.

He blew the whistle again, twice. Lucy stood by the lanyard, hoping it had to be blown again.

"Twice more," said Captain Ming. "Gentle and long."

Lucy tugged the
lanyard twice, slowly, like
a sailor. Like a captain.

On the deck, the
piper got back into full
blast again. The people
looked out for the land.

"They came for the
free trip," said Captain
Ming. "But it will cost
them more to get back
than the amount they've
saved, and they would
not have come this way
at all if the puffer had not

been coming this way, but that's folk for
you, free things at whatever cost. Now,
the two of you, away to the stern, and
when we're alongside the stage throw
out the rope. You've seen it done many
a time, Morag. I'll manage better on the
bridge alone."

The puffer slowed, and crept alongside a little landing stage as neatly as parking a car, water rustling in the paddles, no more noisy than a washing machine chuckling to itself.

Morag threw the rope. The puffer stopped, tied to the land, and sent a jet of steam into the air. Drops of water fell and splashed like rain. A gangplank went down, and the piper marched off, followed by the passengers, to two waiting coaches.

"That din is over," said Lucy. She thought one squeal was very like another.

"He was not doing badly," said Morag. "You should hear Captain Ming if you want to know how never to do it. He is severely bad."

Some trippers and a boy drove into the village and pointed to the puffer. Morag waved and the child waved back.

Lucy kept behind a piece of ship,
because the child looked like Craig –
who was in Cornwall, miles away, surely?

The puffer paddled itself back into
the loch, whistled, and set off again.

"That boy waved," said Morag.
"Did he know you?"

"It couldn't have been me," said
Lucy, thinking of Craig. "And it couldn't
have been him."

"Now we'll find somewhere to
sleep," said Morag. "In the ladies' cabin
we can have a toilet each."

The cabin was a shelter for
passengers on wet days. It was dirty,
like a bus shelter.

"We're the crew now," said Morag.
"We'll get the hosepipe and wash it out."

I should just be sailing, sailing,
Lucy thought. But she put on her boots
and helped to hose the cabin out, and
the deck, the ladies' and the men's

toilets, working their way to the front of
the puffer, and leaving everything clean
but wet.

When they looked beyond the
puffer again there was no lake. The
paddles were turning busily, pit-pat,
pit-pat, the engine cranking and puffing,
but the steamer was moving among the
trees of a forest. The tall funnel caught
on branches, and leaves littered the
freshly swilled deck.

The land was near, and no water
could be seen.

A branch was ripped from its tree overhead and fell into the river. Leaves showered down. Captain Ming on the bridge, steering, was not at all bothered about the shipwreck about to happen, and gently whistled a bagpipe tune to himself.

"He must have seen the mermaid and just be thinking of her," said Morag. "We're too late."

SEVEN

Lucy went back to the cabin and gathered her things together. She knew it was what you did in a shipwreck. Then, when the helicopter comes, they hand your luggage to you, and it goes with your broken leg to the hospital, where you are very brave and you are not going to say anything about it.

"He isn't thinking where we are going," said Morag. "I don't believe in things unless I see them, and other people shouldn't see them either."

Lucy knew she was being told the rules, that she was not ever to have seen Kelpie, and must not ever see the mermaid, though that was why Morag had invited her. Even when Craig helped her he had said at once that there was no such thing as Kelpie, and who ever heard of a water-horse?

After a time when nothing happened except the cracking of branches and more falling leaves, Morag said, "We haven't been shipwrecked yet. The trees overhang the river and got caught on the funnel."

"You don't believe in mermaids," said Lucy.

"That could be it," said Morag, "But if Captain Ming has seen her, we still have a problem."

Captain Ming stopped whistling.

There was a short honk from the puffer's whistle, and he shouted.

"Away there, Morag," he called, leaning over the edge of the bridge. "Are ye doing nothing to earn your passage? It's time to bring the Captain a sup of tea. Away and see Lachlan and find the pot, and make mine black and dark and stiff wi' sugar."

"Not sinking," said Morag.

Lucy took her backpack to the cabin. A ship, she thought, is not complete without a shipwreck.

Beside the richly smelly engine, Lachlan opened the cock for boiling water and Morag filled the pot over four tea-bags. Lachlan went on talking, and going round with his oilcan. Some of the talk was to the engine, and some was to Morag.

Lucy could not understand a word of it. It seemed to be in another language.

Morag could sort out the words, but did not know what they meant.

"It's a side-lever engine," she told Lucy.

"Oh," said Lucy, not knowing either.

"A hundred and fifty years old," said Morag.

Lucy nodded. The engine looked even older.

Lachlan opened a door into a cupboard of flames and threw coal into the fire. Smoke billowed out and caught Lucy's throat.

"Converted to tubes," said Morag.

"Aye," said Lachlan.

Lucy said "Oh," again, but more politely, because Lachlan had told her.

Lachlan told her about the times the engine had been made and mended and improved, until Morag poured four lots of tea and gave him one. "We have to take some to Captain Ming," she said.

"Thank you for showing us your engine."

"It is very nice," said Lucy. "And warm." The engine room was as hot as summer in Spain, where she once had a holiday, she told Lachlan.

"Spain!" said Lachlan, not thinking much of it, opening the fire door and spitting into the fire, while Morag and Lucy climbed the ladder to the deck with three mugs of tea.

"He's been everywhere in the world, but he didn't look at the places and spent all his time in the engine room," said Morag. "That's home to him."

Captain Ming invited them on to the bridge. From here it was clear what was happening. The puffer was going very slowly along a wide river through a forest. There were no trees overhead now.

"There was an island to creep past," said Captain Ming, "where the trees hang across to the water. No, we're not aboot to wreck oursel's on anything."

"Lucy wondered," said Morag.

"Then can I steer?" asked Lucy. She knew she could do that, but was not sure about the whistling.

"You steer too straight," said Captain Ming. "I'll hae to do this part, for I'm using the rudder some of the time, and steering wi' the paddles other times, and the rest is in the hand of Providence."

He drank down his tea as it steamed. Lucy left hers for a very long time, until she could hold the mug without scorching her hands.

"There's more sailing ahead," said Captain Ming at last, "and maybe boats on the water. Ye could keep an eye out forrad and aft, and call out if ye see anything."

"We'll take turns," said Morag.

"I'll look out at the front first, and Lucy over the back."

"What does he expect us to see?" said Lucy. "The mermaid?"

"She goes from his mind until he sees her," said Morag. "Then he has an attack of love at first sight, and he can't guard against it because he doesn't know. Tell me first, if you see her."

Morag did not believe in the mermaid, Lucy remembered, looking out from the back of the puffer.

There was something following them. Lucy thought she was about to see Kelpie and her heart went flip for a second, and then went flop back into its place.

It was not Kelpie, or a mermaid, but the puffer's empty rowing boat, painted blue, at the end of a rope, like a dog on a lead. Lucy had seen it before, but forgotten it.

The river moved slowly under the end of the puffer, and the trees of the forest seemed to follow. It was a wild place, with deer under clearings, no sound anywhere, empty and lonely. The river became wider and the trees further away on either side. Lucy had only the dreaming boat for company. She went to change places with Morag, bored with being alone.

"I nearly came for you," said Morag.

"I was lonely," said Lucy. "That's why I came."

"I wanted you to see this," said Morag. "I never saw anything like it."

Ahead of them a loch was beginning. It was perfectly calm and

completely flat, like a field, and the surface was covered in leaves and flowers.

Being at the very front of the vessel was like flying over a garden. This part of the loch was all growing. As they rode through it and looked over the side, the water showed through like a silver skin.

Lucy was reminded of Kelpie's bridle, the same silvery sheen lying among the stems of grass and flowers. "Is it like this all the way?" she asked, and Morag did not want to say yes or no.

There were birds flying below, fish under the water, shining flies swooping and hovering.

"It's real as well as imaginary," said Morag. "I shan't ever see anything so wonderful. I want to be down there in it."

"The paddle wheels would grind you," said Lucy.

Captain Ming sounded the whistle three times, loudly and suddenly, and broke everything up. A thousand birds flew away, a shadow dropped across the sun, the fish turned and dived, and the shining flies turned drab and dismal.

There was a shout from across the water, another bellow from the puffer, a call from Captain Ming to Lachlan, and the paddles began to move faster.

The magic time had been broken, and died.

Minutes later the puffer was near the shore. Captain Ming had come down from the bridge. A man in a boat had caught a rope thrown to him, and tied it to a black metal bubble floating on the water.

"It's there just for that," said Captain Ming, "every seven years going, and coming back."

Lachlan shut the engine down, and steam began to escape. Captain Ming went to the back of the puffer and led the rowing boat round to the side.

"Down the ladder, you lassies," he said. "We're away to the shore for our dinners, for we've no provisions on board."

EIGHT

Captain Ming unrolled a bundle of string and wood over the rail round the deck. It hung down, but it was still string and wood, rattling against the side of the puffer, dangling into the rowing boat.

"Doon the rope ladder," said Captain Ming.

"Wait a moment," said Morag. "Captain Ming, you know what my mother said about the rowing boat."

"Aye, weel I hadn't been going to trouble," said Captain Ming, "for that little distance."

"I'll get them," said Morag. "Wait here, Lucy."

Lucy peeped over the side. The rope ladder started below the rail, too low to get on, too high above the water and about as sturdy as infant knitting. She decided to stay on board, unless Morag brought something better, like a staircase. Morag brought two red life jackets, for Lucy and herself. Captain Ming and Lachlan went as they were, in overalls.

They waited for Lucy to climb down into the boat, but she could not say a word, or move.

"Ye're safe noo," said Captain Ming. "Morag was up and doon like a wee monkey before she could talk."

Lachlan went first and held the foot of the ladder.

Morag led
Lucy down rung by
rung, working her
wrists and ankles
for her. Lucy closed
her eyes, feeling
the slow sway of
the puffer under
her hands, and the
jiggling of the
rowing boat under
her feet.

Captain Ming
stood in the stern
of the rowing boat,
and rowed them to
the land with one oar. Lucy said she
wondered why Morag had been so fussy
about life-jackets, when they didn't sink
after all.

"But you don't know when it will
be," said Morag.

"Hmph," said Captain Ming, who couldn't swim fifty metres, he said, nor know a metre if he met one.

They had their meal with cousins of Captain Ming and Mrs MacAlister, who ran a small bed and breakfast hotel. Captain Ming told Lucy and Morag to eat large and fast, because they must be away soon, down the river as far as they could get, to meet the tide where the river joined the firth, with no time for meals on the puffer.

"There's a sandbar," he said. "The tide in the firth has to lift high and hold the river back, so that we can cross over in the middle of the day tomorrow. The puffer can only get repaired when the tide and the river are right."

And when it's broken, Lucy thought.

"The river has to be full," said Captain Ming. "We go a day or two before the full moon, and back a day or two after, to fit the tides."

Lucy nodded her head. She knew about tides and moons from being at the seaside in Lyme Regis with the sea going out and in, leaving golden fossils on the beach. But for now she was being offered more pudding and Morag was pouring custard for her.

Lucy wondered whether to sign the visitors' book, as they went by it on the way out. When she saw the open page she decided not to, because of what was in there already. "Craig," it said, with more people of the same surname, probably his parents. Lucy did not know their first names. Craig was enough, even if it was some other person, not the one she knew. She closed the book and walked on.

Captain Ming pushed against the sandy beach until the water was deep enough among the waterweeds to row in, with the fish moving below in the water.

All through her dinner Lucy had practised climbing up the rope ladder. Now she was not thinking about it, but hoping no Craig was anywhere near, it was quite easy. Morag saw she was thoughtful and asked her whether she was all right. "Nearly at the top," Lucy said.

She was first on deck, and saw the mermaid in the water, looking at the puffer.

The mermaid pushed long wet yellow hair back from her face with both hands. I shall see her tail, Lucy thought. To prove it's her.

The mermaid waved. Lucy knew she had another duty, and ignored the wave.

She wanted to wave and shout,

throw off the life-jacket, join the mermaid in the water and learn about living there. She took off the life-jacket but she knew they had failed, and that Captain Ming was lost.

"What's the matter?" asked Morag, coming up the rope ladder next.

Captain Ming was still in the rowing boat, calling across to the mermaid. She was calling back to him. Morag was waving to her, even though Lucy pulled at her arm to stop her.

"It's Kathryn," said Morag. "She's at my school, the Academy, and lives over here. She's swum out to untie the rope so we can get away."

"Oh," said Lucy. "I thought it was the mermaid."

Most people would have laughed at Lucy. Morag was more thoughtful, and more careful. She had another look at the swimmer in the water.

"It's Kathryn, I'm sure," she said. "You'll know the mermaid, because," and, as Captain Ming came on deck behind her, she whispered a strange thing for someone who did not believe in mermaids, "she has green hair."

Captain Ming went up to the bridge. Lachlan tied the rowing boat to the stern of the puffer, and came back to his engine room. The paddles twitched, pit-pat as they caught the water. The puffer turned from the land. Captain Ming sounded the whistle. Kathryn untied the rope. Morag hauled the loose end up out of the water and left it in a leafy puddle on the deck. Lucy waved to Kathryn, and Kathryn swam away.

"She does not want to be among the paddles," said Morag. "For-by she would break them. They are a strong people down the river here. You should see her toss the caber at the school games."

The puffer left the loch, and the river closed in again. There were few trees, and the river went through rocky places, wilder than field or forest. Once there were cliffs either side, another

time green soft land with hundreds of ponds in it, or spiky hills with animals. Morag said they were goats.

The puffer stayed neatly astride the middle of the river. It was hard for Captain Ming to find the middle, and he would not have visitors on the bridge.

He called for tea at the end of the afternoon, and again when darkness fell. Lachlan came up on deck to argue about where they were. Each of them thought the other had forgotten the way, or never known it.

"Ye're away beyont it, mon," Lachlan said.

"It's anither mile," said Captain Ming.

"We'll be on our side in the firth any minute," said Lachlan. "And then who knew where he was, eh?"

In the end they both saw what they were looking for, brought the puffer alongside a little landing stage, and tied up in complete darkness all round, then lit happy electric lights all over the puffer.

They went to sleep in deep black night. A high bird yodelled among the stars, and flew over the edge of the world. It was a sad sound, but Lucy felt full of joy at hearing it. What voice? she wondered. The mermaid? Wolves? But she was asleep before she worked it out.

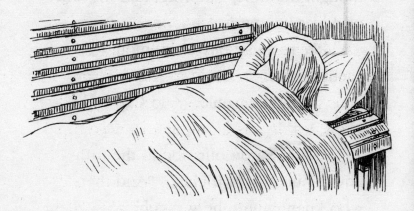

NINE

Lucy was cold, and everything was dark and noisy. Something was scratching and scraping almost underneath her, biting the puffer, she thought, hearing its teeth going through the sides. It was a time not to wake up, because it was all not a dream.

The biting stopped. There was a hefty clanging thud, and Lucy knew that Lachlan had closed the fire door of the engine. There was a smell of engine room, and a sooty hiss of steam. It was safe to wake up, but she went back to sleep, still not very warm.

She woke again with daylight just beginning to show in the cabin. She was on the floor, or deck, and Morag was sitting up and looking at her.

"Have you broken your leg?" she asked. "Falling from your bed like Granny MacAlister?"

"No," said Lucy, moving her toes. "I fell awake, that's all. I've been hearing wolves."

"It was a wild cat," said Morag.

By the time they got up the puffer was moving again. Lachlan said there was enough fire to grill bacon. Morag made sandwiches of that, with a great deal of mustard for Captain Ming.

"Eat up," he said. "There'll be no dinner the day until we tie up in Glasgow. So put on your life-jackets, and dinna fret Lachlan or me. Look out at the bow, and sing out if you see ae thing strange."

The river grew wider and faster, where a tributary joined, the water one side clear, on the other dark with mud and sand.

"It will have been raining up in the mountains," said Morag. "The boat floats differently."

Lucy's bacon sandwich felt the difference, wished it had not been eaten and thought about coming back. The puffer swayed gently from side to side.

"Is that something swimming?" said Morag, trying to take Lucy's mind away from its wobbly feeling.

"Has it got green hair?" Lucy asked, being kind back, and hoping the sandwich felt the same.

"Yes," said Morag. She shouted up to the bridge. "A big log coming by on the right side," and pointed. A broken tree with trailing leaves came down the clear river, lifting its head, looking at everything.

Captain Ming blew the whistle. The puffer turned away from the tree and gave it room to go ahead.

"The mermaid will be something like that," said Morag. "He will have fallen in love with a lump of wood. But he doesn't think that one is it."

Captain Ming shouted to Lachlan. The puffer's paddles stopped. The puffer went on just as fast, floating on live water. Lachlan came up to the bridge and looked at the water with Captain Ming. They both nodded their heads, and then shook them.

Captain Ming came down to look at things in the water. "We'll turn and come round again," he said. "We're early for the sea wave over the bar. When there is a wee white line in the distance, by the time we get to it it'll be the deep water we want."

The puffer turned and went upstream again. It turned again and went towards the sandbar, through rough water where the rivers mingled.

The surface of the river stopped shining. Lucy did not think it mattered, only that there was more mud. But rain was falling, at first a drizzle, and then a shower, and at last a downpour. There was so much rain that Lucy could not see land either side or ahead. Morag fetched a smelly piece of canvas and draped it over both of them in the bow.

"If I could remember what it looked like," Lucy told Morag, "I might be able to see it better."

"Every bit helps," said Captain Ming. "Keep an eye out for that wave. It'll come, but we canna time it to the minute. The deeper the water at the bar the better it is to cross."

There was only water below, rain above it, grey rain all round, and nothing else to be seen.

"How can he tell where to go?" said Morag.

"It's all right," said Lucy. "I'm feeling a bit sick again, so we're in the rough bit in the middle."

"It's you that has the rough bit in the middle," said Morag. "Isn't it?"

Something licked the backs of their necks, warm through the wet canvas. The cloud had gone away and the sun had leapt out and dropped on them.

The veil of rain went away across the water, and the land appeared again to either side.

Ahead, sparkling in the sunlight, was the wave they wanted, a straight white line.

"The wave," Morag shouted, turning towards the bridge. Lucy turned with her, and sunshine leapt into her eyes, turning everything red. The whistle sounded. The paddles raced. There was steam roaring up the funnel. The deck trembled.

"Steady," shouted Captain Ming. "Hold tight, lassies. She'll lift, she'll lift."

The wave came towards them, white at the crest, deeply muddy below, across the river like a fence.
"It's standing on the bar," shouted Captain Ming. "We're going through."

The bow kicked up, and shook from side to side. Water boiled round the paddles and churned in the covers above them. The puffer waggled her tail like a duck, seemed to jump the fence of foam, then sat like a swan, still and steady in water that looked smooth but was full of movement. There was a wind after the rain, a smell of salt, and the calling of gulls.

"The sea," said Morag. "And in the sea is the mermaid."

"But you don't believe in her," said Lucy.

"I haven't seen her hair," said Morag. "But I've seen her tail. Look."

In the waves something swam. It might have green hair, but it put its head in the water and did a somersault. It had a tail like a fish.

"He's sure to see it," said Lucy. Then she thought for a moment. "But what's wrong with that, really?" she asked. Captain Ming could surely do as he liked, and so could the mermaid.

"We'd never hear the last of it, that's what," said Morag. "If he falls in love with her again it's pathetic, since she doesn't exist. That's a seal, not a mermaid. And they have very bad fishy breath."

"Mermaids?" asked Lucy. "You must

have seen one to know its natural history."

"Seals," said Morag. "Mermaids have good breath. They sing, and I'll prove it, because people have often not heard them. How could they?"

Lucy thought this was a backwards proof. Of course people have not often heard mermaids, yet they must exist or Mum would not have believed a story about Captain Ming and his sweetheart.

I shall know by the not very bad fishy breath.

TEN

The puffer was sailing very freely now. Lachlan came up from the engine room and looked round.

"Aye," he said. "She'll run. All we have to think of is the trip back again."

Captain Ming said it was time for tea all round.

The puffer was in open water, with land getting further away on either side. This was not the loch the puffer lived on, where the wind blew up a few wriggly waves. This was not the bumpy but short journey across the bar. The wide water had come up with the tide, and brought with it the sway of the sea. The sway got into the deck.

Lucy thought it might be better to hold on to the rail. "I'll think about things," she said. "You do the tea. I'll watch out for you-know-what."

"Seals?" said Morag, and left her.

My head is moving about, thought Lucy, and I'm cold and I've got nothing to do. And if I had something to do I wouldn't be able to. She wished the paddles would not go "Pit pat, gurgle, slop," in a happy but selfish way under her feet.

Morag came back into those thoughts, which had gone round and round in Lucy's head like dizziness. "Wrap this round you like Granny MacAlister's shawl," she said, hanging

the canvas round Lucy's shoulders. She
went off to the engine room to make tea.

Lucy felt better at once, almost all
the way through, and decided that the
deck of the puffer was a safe place to be,
and was beginning to be comfortable,
when someone looked at her.

Lucy had not been looking at anything, but when something looked she knew at once, without knowing what had looked, or where it was. It had not merely seen her, but looked.

It was not a thing. It was a she. She had swum up the water towards the puffer, lifted her body from the water, raised a hand to her eyes, and made a careful observation that included Lucy.

Lucy searched the grey water until she saw green hair.

The mermaid took her hand from her eyes and waved her arm, looking no longer at Lucy, but higher up.

Above Lucy's head Captain Ming was on the bridge. He looked down at Lucy. "Are ye well?" he asked.

"Yes," said Lucy, at once, used to the feelings of moving deck. "Thank you. And how are you?"

"Busy," said Captain Ming. "Away up on the bridge and steer. Ye ken how to do it, do ye not?"

Lucy thought she should speak to Morag first. But the thought of the engine room, with its steam and oiliness, was still too much for her. She dropped the canvas and went up the bridge ladder.

"Steer towards that flashing light on the tower," said Captain Ming. The tower and the light were a long way ahead, rising from a heap of rocks at the water's edge.

"In the rocks," said Lucy.

"Rocks?" said Captain Ming. "That's

the houses of town, a way off yet. Steady ahead while I get the binoculars from below."

He went down the ladder and towards his little office. If he went to the rail, just in front of the paddle casing, Lucy saw, he need only glance over to see the mermaid. She was still alongside the puffer now, without getting nearer, and was watching it.

He'll know when he's looked at, Lucy thought.

She attended to her job, and found she was not steering straight towards the tower and its light. Like a bicycle, she thought. You don't draw a line between the front wheel and the place you are going. You just look there and go there.

Captain Ming found his binoculars, and stayed on the deck below to use them, looking ahead.

Lucy held the wheel firmly, and

turned her head to see the mermaid off to the right.

The mermaid was not there. She had not looked at Captain Ming. He had not seen her.

Just imagination, thought Lucy. To make sure she turned her head to look back, to where the wake lay tumbled but straight on the water.

The mermaid was following in the middle of the wake, swimming gently, looking at the puffer.

She knows it, thought Lucy. She will know all the ships that come here. But she only cares about one person on board one ship.

That person, Captain Ming, was now coming up the ladder. Morag followed him, carrying his mug of tea.

"Hot?" he said. "Dark as treacle, is it?"

And Lucy was saying, "Am I going towards the right place?" because she wanted Captain Ming to look to the front, not behind.

"Just blaw the whustle two times," said Captain Ming. "Then listen for a reply." He looked and listened ahead. Lucy pulled the lanyard and sounded the whistle twice.

The sound bounced back gently from the land many a fading time. Captain Ming listened ahead.

Two sounds came from there, like dogs barking.

"Aye," said Captain Ming drinking his tea slowly for once, and rubbing the back of his neck. "The tug is on the way to pull us to the shipyard. We've done our journey, with no trouble at all. Is Lachlan needing me I wonder, or was it just a feeling? Stay on course, lassies. If ye need me pull the whustle." He drained his mug, and went down the ladder thoughtfully.

When he had gone Lucy spoke. "Look back and you'll see her," she said. "She looked at me, and she's looked at Captain Ming, because I felt it."

"I feel something," said Morag, looking ahead, steering. "But it's my dinner I'm wanting." She turned her head only enough to give Lucy a sweet smile, to show that imaginary beings were imaginary. So far, at any rate.

ELEVEN

Lucy put one hand on the wheel. She had to make Morag turn and look. "I'll keep it still," she said. "You turn your head . . ." She did not finish the words, because there was no reason for Morag to turn her head. The mermaid was no longer enjoying the run of the wake behind the puffer.

"Aye?" said Morag. "And what will I see?"

"If you won't look," said Lucy, "you

won't see. You just don't want to, and that's why you won't; but if she isn't nonsense then it's sense to see her."

"I didn't see her," said Morag. "It's as good as nonsense, Lucy."

At school Craig teased Lucy, not always very kindly. Elspbeth said that Craig really admired her but couldn't find out how to say so. Lucy did not find anything to admire in Craig, who turned everything she said into its opposite, shouted that Lucy could not be right about anything, and made a disagreeable face at the same time.

Now Morag was insisting that Lucy was not right about something important to them all. She was not shouting, but the result was still disagreeable. Lucy thought, We came on the puffer to keep Captain Ming and the mermaid apart. Now she's here and Morag is the only one who can do anything, but I am the one who has seen the mermaid, who has already looked at Captain Ming. Now he has gone to the engine room to think about it.

"You should look," Lucy told Morag.

"Havers," said Morag, meaning 'Nonsense.'

"But," said Lucy, "that's why we are here."

"Such a tale," said Morag. She was not making faces at Lucy, but staring very hard ahead. You have to if you are steering a straight wake; or if you are not going to change your mind about something.

"Then what you said was not true," said Lucy. "If it's not true then it's a lie."

Morag held the wheel more tightly. She looked even harder ahead. "I'm busy," she said, "or I could explain things."

"You couldn't," said Lucy. "You will never explain anything to me, Morag MacAlister."

She would have stamped her foot, but only little ones do that. She would have cried, but only infants do that. She would have screamed, but only babies do that. She turned away and looked at the water.

The mermaid was clearly there, swimming, then stopping and looking back, swimming again, her head above the water, little waves breaking into foam against her, a wake showing behind her.

"There," said Lucy. "There she is. Morag, look. Look, look, look, look."

Morag looked. "I see nothing," she said. "Weel, there is something. It'll be a duck, that's all."

"With long green hair?" said Lucy.

"It's what they have in old stories," said Morag.

However, she went on looking. The wake of puffer began to curve.

Captain Ming was out of the engine room at once and up the ladder to the bridge. "Morag," he said, "you ken better than that how to steer the ship."

"Sorry," said Morag. "I was thinking of something else."

"But the Captain carries the blame," said Captain Ming, taking the wheel from her. "We don't want to run aground in sight of our destination, or anywhere, for that matter."

Morag looked out across the water still. Lucy looked with her. There was no sign of the mermaid in the moving water.

Lucy said, "I thought I saw the Loch Ness Monster, and we steered round it."

"Something like that," said Morag.

"Away with your fancies, the pair of you," said Captain Ming. "Go and get warm in the engine room."

Morag took a long last look over the water. Lucy looked with her, and saw nothing.

"Watch as ye go," said Captain Ming. "The water is getting lively."

Lucy had to hold with both hands on the way to the deck, and the deck itself kept tipping over.

But now Lucy did not mind at all. She followed Morag down the ladder into the engine room. Lachlan was tapping a brass gauge to check his steam pressure.

It had been cold on the bridge. It was comfortably warm here, and smells of oil and coal and steam were part of the comfort.

Lachlan said, "If you look in yonder box, Morag, there's shortbreads my mither made. I dunk them in hot water and get both food and drink that way."

They sat round in the warm engine

room, dipping shortbread in a mug of hot engine water.

A bell rang. The whistle blew twice.

"We've to stop engines," said Lachlan. He pulled levers and the paddles became still. Captain Ming blew the whistle again. Lachlan turned a wheel round. Steam escaped outside. The engine stopped turning.

"Standstill," said Lachlan. "What is he doing?"

The puffer was not going forwards or backwards. Waves rocked it gently. Lucy sucked her shortbread and stayed where she was. Lachlan wiped his hands on a rag and went up to see what Captain Ming wanted.

"He's seen her," said Lucy, realizing what might have happened.

Morag stood up. She sat down. "Havers," she said. She stood up again. "We'd best go and see."

"So you do believe," said Lucy.

"It's what he believes that matters," said Morag. "You know what I think." She went up to the deck.

Lucy stayed to finish the shortbread, and wondered why Morag was making such a noise. The mermaid is on board, she thought. She stood up, banged her head on some pipes, and went to see what was what.

There was no mermaid. Sitting together on the deck were two solemn little boys. Skipping about was a slightly bigger girl, shouting excitedly at Captain Ming, but not in words that Lucy understood. A bigger boy was talking to Lachlan. A girl between the ages of Lucy and Morag was talking to Morag. Captain Ming was talking to a woman and holding a large baby.

"Granny MacAlister is well," he told Morag.

"We have heard each day," said the woman.

"Auntie Shona," said Morag. "This is Lucy, and Lucy, this is the new baby. She weighed ten pounds when she was born, and she is my cousin, and she is called Bonnie Bluebell Blithe, and this is Rosie, and that's John Willie, and next is Poppy, and the wee boys are Charley and Teddy and that's Auntie Shona."

Captain Ming handed the baby to Morag. "Hold fast," he said. "She has an unco amount of gravity."

"The mermaid came and told us you were out here," said Poppy, nodding her head so that everyone knew how true it was. "He's in love with her, you know."

"She sang to us," said Rosie. "We were expecting her. Now you're to come with us for dinner while Captain Ming and Lachlan are off to the dock."

TWELVE

Lucy had only climbed the rope ladder in a calm loch. Now the puffer lifted up and down, and a boat at its foot moved like a see-saw with two middles.

Auntie Shona went straight down the ladder. Morag slung her and Lucy's luggage on a rope, and Lucy followed with her own hands and feet.

In the boat one knee wanted to kick her chin, and the other to leave her

entirely. Captain Ming brought the baby.
Two boys tried to manage alone.

"They'll get cross," said Rosie.

"Aye," said Captain Ming, who was
bringing them down fighting against
being helped. "Ye wouldna!"

"I will, so," said the wee boys,
fighting harder.

Auntie Shona started the outboard
motor, and the boat moved away from
the puffer. The puffer blew its whistle,
and smoke poured hissingly from the
funnel.

The paddles scratched the water,
pit-pat, pit-pat, and she moved on.

It was not dinner time on land, but
tea. Lucy fell asleep at the table with her
mouth full.

In the morning her bed crawled with
babies of all sizes, Teddy and Charlie and
Bonnie and Poppy, all of them talking.
She could not understand them.

"I can't even make those sounds,"
she told Morag.

"It's engineering," said Morag. "All
engineers."

"Ships' engines," said John Willie,
building a new kind on the floor.

They went to the dock later on,
and looked at an engine of the old kind.
The puffer was in a dry dock, held up
with beams of wood. The deck was up,
the funnel was off, the paddles were
showing.

Men hammered and measured,
banged and scraped, sawed and sparked
all over her. It was the two-million mile

service, Lachlan explained, keeping an eye on his engine. Last time they had wanted to put new gauges and dials on, but he would not let them.

Auntie Shona took crawling babies from among wheels and pistons where they had managed to get black engineering grease on themselves.

"It's in the family," said Auntie Shona, when Lucy was helping to bath them later on. "Don't trouble to wash it off; it'll sink in and be gone."

They went into town the next day, to look at all the special sights. Everybody wore kilts, with one of Rosie's for Lucy. The little ones had plastic baggy knickers underneath theirs, trailing through markets and cathedrals, and stealing toys at a museum.

Once in the crowd Lucy heard someone call her name, but she did not see who it was.

"A mermaid, no doubt," said Morag.

On the next visit to the puffer Lucy thought it might not come together in time. On the next she was sure it wouldn't, ever. The third time there was a stack of pieces that had been forgotten about.

"It's no' richt," Lachlan was saying. "It's no' richt." The engineers put in new parts and ignored him. John Willie studied the matter with Lachlan, but they ended shaking their heads in disagreement.

Rosie and John Willie took Lucy and Morag fishing, in their boat but not a great way from land.

"She sat on that rock," said Rosie, undoing the mooring rope when Morag had pulled the engine alive. "And sang to us."

"I heard her," said John Willie. Engineers know.

"She doesn't have words," said Rosie. "It was all sad, and glad, and lamenting for things."

Morag steered them away from the rock, disbelieving in mermaids and where they had been.

"She was there," said Rosie.

"I said they were great teases," said Morag.

They caught one of Lucy's socks, but no fishes.

"But they're being called to us," said John Willie. He cocked his ear and listened. Rosie put a finger to her lips and opened her eyes wide.

Morag turned her head, and stopped listening, though it was clear she had heard the same song coming across the water. There were no words to it, and that meant one particular singer was singing.

Lucy looked round. She saw mermaid

everywhere, and nowhere too. Her eyes made her out of a rock, or a ripple, or a shadow from a cloud.

"It'll be the kirk bells," said Morag, and she stopped looking.

"On a Thursday," said Rosie. "Never."

Where she might be expected, thought Lucy, looking more calmly round her, she has appeared. "Sitting on the rock," she said. "Look to one side."

"Yes," said Rosie, "that's her."

"Calling the fish," said John Willie.

"It's something on the shore beyond," said Morag, glancing quickly. "You only see it when you look past it because of the focus. A sort of blue."

"With green hair?" said Lucy. "And singing?"

"A tree," said Morag. "An echo."

At that moment John Willie caught a big fish, and needed help. Morag also had one. Lucy's line tightened, and she brought in a fish that bubbled at her.

The singing was over, and the mermaid had gone.

"We drifted away from the rock that's got things that look like themselves but they aren't," said Morag. "That's all. And the more people who don't see her, the less likely it is that Captain Ming will."

"It's a family thing," said John Willie. "I don't fancy love or green hair, so I'm all right."

"If we've seen her it's true," said Lucy.

"It's only as true as we make it," said Morag, tugging at the motor to start it. "The best way to make it right is not to believe."

"She's difficult about Santa Claus too," said Rosie.

THIRTEEN

Two fish were baked for tea, and one frozen for later teas. Lucy was possibly eating the first thing she had ever caught and killed.

Was the second thing to be a mermaid, when she stopped believing in her?

After tea Mum was on the telephone, to see how she was getting on.

"I'm holding the baby," said Lucy, sitting with Bonnie on her knee. "It's huge. Yes, fine Mum. Fishing for tea.

I caught my own sock. Of course not,
only the fish. In the Toy Museum
yesterday the boy babies wanted to steal
the toys. No, Morag says we haven't,
and I don't believe in it any more.
Tomorrow we go to an island. No, I felt
like it but I never was and I won't be.
Poppy wants to say hello."

Poppy muttered things that no one
could understand, then shrieked loudly.
Mum said that Lucy seemed to be in
good hands for now, and see you on
Sunday, and that was the end of the call.

In the morning the dry dock was
filling with water round the puffer. Smoke
came from the funnel, and Lachlan sat
on the deck eating a pie. Men from the
dockyard were on board to keep an eye
on things during the sea trial.

The puffer was as firm as a
building under their feet when Lucy
went on board.

Morag stamped her feet. "It's like a rock," she said.

"She's still in the cradle," Captain Ming said. "Not afloat yet. She'll lift any time."

"No one can fall off," said Auntie Shona, letting the twins run about the deck. They sat down together, because the bows had lifted.

A crane pulled the cradle away, and large wood floated on the water. The gates were opened fully, ready for the puffer to be pulled out by a black tug, towed to the middle of the firth, and let go. The tug honked. The puffer whistled. Seagulls shouted back.

The paddles moved. The puffer began to leave a wake as she went gently past the whole town, whistling at huge ferries that visited other lands, at fishermen, at sailing boats and colliers, at container ships and tankers. She went under bridges and alongside floating buoys big enough to live in, with lights and bells on.

The engines moved faster. The land fell away behind them and the sea was empty ahead. The deck lifted and subsided. Twins fell over again and again. Splashes of salt water came on board, and there was mist round the paddle-casings.

John Willie came out of the engine room, carrying a long oil can. "We're busy," he said.

There was a sea breeze on deck, but sunshine with it. Auntie Shona sat everyone below the rail, out of the wind, and brought out the sandwiches.

"One missing," she said, counting them.

"Mermaid," said Poppy.

"It's my oily boy," said Auntie Shona. "He'll take his dinner back to the engine room."

The wind came round a different way, and they had to move to another shelter further along the rail.

There was moving sea all round. Faransay was grey, but turned green as they came near, with cliffs and beaches, sheep on the hills, and a white house by a jetty. Seabird shouts scratched the sky.

Eanster separated from Faransay. Clowder was a lonely rock beyond that, and waves jumped over it.

"There is never a calm here," said Auntie Shona. "Landing here is desperate."

"I wouldn't land," said Lucy, looking at the rocks and the waves foaming white. "There are maggots."

The maggots lifted their heads and looked back at Lucy. It was not like being looked at by a mermaid.

"Not maggots," said Auntie Shona, "but seals, further off than you think."

The puffer circled Clowder and went down the far side of Eanster and Faransay. Halfway along the long low side of Eanster, where the sea climbs the sloping rock for ever, Lucy knew she was being looked at.

Captain Ming felt it too. He blew the whistle.

"Answering," said Lucy. She could not see where the mermaid was, but she knew she was there, and searching for Captain Ming.

Morag did not see anything either. "When I was about five years old," she said, "they told me I had seen it. But I don't believe myself all the time."

Lachlan came out of the engine room and called up to the bridge to know what the whistle meant, and was he to go faster or slower.

"Neither," said Captain Ming.

"That's best," said Lachlan, looking

at the island, going back to his engine, shaking his head.

It doesn't matter what I do, thought Lucy. He answered her. Why shouldn't he fall in love and go to the island, if that is where he belongs?

Lucy, Rosie, and Morag, were at the stern, looking back at the wake. In that wake something swam with arms and tail, coming closer and closer.

"Well?" said Rosie. "She's there, isn't she?"

A hand held on to the rowing boat in the foam.

"Webbed fingers like an otter," said Rosie.

"Don't encourage her," said Morag. "It's fancy."

Lucy could see plainly what was plainly there, "Morag," she said firmly, "I believe what I see."

"You see what you believe," said Morag.

"I'll get Mum," said Rosie. "She'll believe what's there. She's sensible nearly all the time."

By the time Auntie Shona got to the stern with the heavy baby, and the twins, the mermaid had gone.

"She maybe forgot him," said Auntie Shona. "And he forgets her. What can you do about love?"

"I'm practising," said Morag. "We must do our best, but if it doesn't work, then that's the way it is to be."

FOURTEEN

aransay, Eanster, but first of all
Clowder, went out of sight. There
was quiet after the shouting gulls.
Lachlan's engine ran with hardly a
sound. Engine smoke lifted from the
funnel and faded in the sky.

The mainland grew nearer. The
puffer came into flat water, with the waves
dying before they reached it. Walking
babies were not falling over so often.

The puffer spent the night tied up

outside the shipyard. There was more work to be done, Morag said, the best part of the next day.

"We go across the bar at midnight, at the full moon," she reminded Lucy.

"You'll be well able to see her," said Rosie.

"That's only a story," said Morag. But all the same, she looked up quickly at Captain Ming, to make sure that so far nothing had come real for him.

Lucy's face had shrunk tight to her bones in the sea wind, and her eyes could not stay open. She yawned her way through tea, and then fell asleep.

"She's dreaming now," she heard Auntie Shona say. "But it's woken her up too."

Then it was morning for Lucy. Twins were climbing on her, her lips tasted of salt, and no one had cleaned her teeth.

The puffer left after tea. Before they left, Lucy was a long time on board helping Lachlan, because of the family goodbyes happening ashore.

"It's a clan," said Lachlan, checking oil boxes over the paddles. "A tribe."

The voyage began at last. Morag and Lucy leaned on the rail and waved at the docksides.

"I'll see them again in summer," said Morag.

"I would like that," said Lucy.

The day turned to dusk. Captain Ming switched on lights, different colours at the sides, and glaring ones at bow and stern. The land was dark either side, with houselights on it, and traffic on a big road. Trains rode by, coughing out of tunnels, calling with horns.

The moon came over the hills, bright as money.

There was music from a party at one of the houses, and reflections of fireworks going down the firth as rockets went up the sky.

"Are you weens not away to your beds?" Captain Ming asked from the bridge.

"We'll help you over the bar first," said Morag.

"It's a wee while yet," said Captain Ming. "So see Lachlan and brew some tea."

Lachlan was pleased with his engine. "She is running very sweet," he said. "The drinking water is too fresh. It will improve with time." The tea did not taste of oil, nor even very much of smoke.

When they had finished it Morag heard music on the water again. This time there were no lights, no house, no fireworks, only a bulging full moon swimming under the waves, and the song.

Lucy knew what it was. "I can hear it too," she said. I will prove it to her, she thought.

"A fisherman out in a boat with a transistor," said Morag. "He will have a light, or the puffer will run him down."

"Whisht there, you lassies," called Captain Ming.

"Not us," Morag called back. "We are just looking for the fisherman's light."

"Where?" asked Captain Ming. "I see nothing."

"There is nothing to see," Morag called.

Captain Ming called back from the bridge, "We are to cross the bar now. It will turn a little rough."

He sounded the whistle. The engine speeded up a little, steam coughing through the funnel. It never went very fast, and only the busier sound of the paddles meant anything.

"Running at it," said Morag, peering over the side. "It's like going uphill a bit, and the tide lifts us. Then goodbye to her. She won't come over the bar. Don't look, Lucy."

The mermaid swam in brilliant electric light.

"You can really see her, Morag," said Lucy.

"That," said Morag, "is lost fish net, no more."

The mermaid had other ideas of reality. She stood high in the water and called out in song.

There was a shout from Captain Ming. He blew the whistle twice. The engine slowed and stopped. The paddles rested. The puffer swung about on the water. The moon shone now from one side, now the other.

"What noo?" shouted Lachlan from the engine room.

"Lachlan," said Morag, "he's seen her. Drive on full speed. We aren't over the bar yet." She did not stop to tell him more, but was up on the bridge, shaking Captain Ming by the sleeve.

"Losh," said Lachlan. "Excuse me. Aye, that I will. But Lucy, one of us had best mind the engine, and the other have words wi' the silkie."

"Silkie?" said Lucy.

"Mermaid," said Lachlan. "Tell her to bide until the next time, and then she can have him."

"But he hasn't to go with her, ever," said Lucy. "So it won't be true."

"This is the last time the puffer will go to the dock," said Lachlan. "In seven years they will send the puffer for scrap. There is no next time, so she can have

him then, and that's not a lie, only what
will not happen."

Captain Ming was calling, "Lead us
ashore, and I will come with you,"
sounding like a song himself. "I will
play the pipes. We shall sing together."

Morag was scolding him, telling
him to get across the bar, and then talk
with the mermaid. "He is not the best
performer," she told Lucy. "You should
be hearing my dad one of these days."

"Lachlan is working the engine,"
said Lucy. "I'll talk to her."

"Do that," Morag shouted. "I'll steer
us over the bar. He'll be safe from her in
the river, and we'll be safe too."

FIFTEEN

With the engine going again the puffer stopped swinging in the water. Lucy ran to the bow and looked over the rail. She thought the mermaid would be there, to stop the puffer going across. She heard her singing somewhere along the side, and went along that way, past the paddles throbbing in their casing, and towards the stern.

"Send her away," Morag shouted, from the wheel.

"We'll go ashore," Captain Ming called, explaining what was bound to happen. "And not over the bar tonight, or any night."

The mermaid sang sweetly back to him. Captain Ming could sense her look. "Now leave me, Morag," he was saying. "This is where I'm bound to be, at the edge of the sea in my own ship. We'll run it on land, and I shall live between the tides, and so can she."

"She's going away," said Morag. "Lucy, tell him she's going away."

"But she isn't," said Lucy, not able to think of anything but the truth, and say it. The mermaid was closer now, beside the stern and looking up, looking up towards Captain Ming.

"You have to go away," Lucy called to her, not shouting, speaking loudly. The mermaid heard. Her singing stopped. She looked at Lucy, and Lucy felt the look. It was not at all kindly or loving, but stubborn and determined, and it hurt.

"Don't do that," said Lucy.

"Drive on shore," said Captain Ming. "I shall stay, and you lassies and Lachlan can go."

Lachlan came up from the engines hastily, to see what was going on, one foot ready to dive back below. He had to know what was happening.

"Nearly there," Morag called, seeing him.

"Nearly on shore," called Captain Ming. "Ye'll get your wage, Lachlan, just tell my sister where I've gone, how long I've waited."

"I'll do that, Captain," said Lachlan. "Just hoot when ye want full power." He came to Lucy and looked over the stern. He saw what the mermaid was doing.

Lucy had not dared hang over far enough to be sure.

"The wee sea-devil is pushing us ashore," he said. "Noo what?" Then he went to the bow and looked ahead, and was back in a moment. He stopped on the way to call to Morag to steer straight as she was.

To Lucy he said loudly, "Aye, we're steering on shore, very weel and briskly. We'll tear the bottom out of her and Captain Ming will be here for good."

The mermaid sang louder. Lachlan bent his head and said to Lucy, "We'll be over the bar in ten minutes, but don't let her think it." He leaned over again and shouted to Lucy, but for the mermaid to hear, "We need all the help we can get to drive the ship right on the rocks so she'll never move again."

It's time for telling lies, thought Lucy. Though a shipwreck would be nice.

Craig would be jealous. They don't have ship crashes in Cornwall.

Lachlan went back to the engine, and the paddles turned faster. The wake rippled in the electric light, but the mermaid was under the overhang of the stern, and Lucy could only hear her singing.

"You're doing it right," Lucy called. "The land is just coming."

On the bridge Morag was talking severely to Captain Ming, but not about mermaids or driving the ship on shore. "That's not the way to fold a shirt," she was telling him. "Don't bundle your socks, pack them flat. You don't need that, she'll like a beard best, and a towel's no use under the water."

"I should have been ready," Captain Ming was saying. "What will she think of me? I am coming," he called, "I am almost ready."

The puffer twitched on the water. The paddles ran heavy where the flood of the river pulled the tide higher over the bar, and the puffer climbed a wave.

Morag blew a long blast on the whistle.

Lucy leaned over as far as she dared. The mermaid looked up to her. "We're doing it," Lucy shouted. "We'll hit land, we'll be on the beach. Push, push."

The mermaid sang happily back, without words.

"Just tuck them under your arm," Morag was saying, when Captain Ming tried to pack the bagpipes.

The puffer twitched again, bobbed left and right, lifted itself, and was out of the tide and into the river, dropping over the bar and away from the sea.

The mermaid stopped singing, all at once.

"We're over the bar now," Captain Ming said, in a normal voice. He had forgotten the mermaid all at once, and was looking round bewildered by his packed bag. "We'll slow down." The whistle blew twice. The paddles stopped bustling round in their casings. Lachlan came out to see how things had gone.

"She jumped more than once," he said.

"There was not so very much water," said Captain Ming. "I wonder whether we didn't touch bottom as we crossed. What were we thinking, to leave it so late?"

Lucy came up to the bridge.

Captain Ming held the wheel now, looking ahead. Morag put the suitcase aside and bundled the bagpipes away.

"He's forgotten," said Lachlan. "She is in his mind no longer. We can be glad of that. She'll be at her island the noo, so it's over with for ever. We'll not mention it and it'll not come again. But you did a grand job, the pair of ye, a great deception."

Captain Ming looked forward beyond the glare of the electric light. "Slow ahead, Lachlan," he said. "We'll tie up on the deep side of the bend yonder."

The puffer shook as it went over the rough join of the two rivers, and settled into the calm flow.

It approached the bank slowly, with Captain Ming calling to Lachlan for more power or less, and ran up against land so gently that a basket of eggs would not have cracked or a jug of milk spilt.

Lachlan tied the stern to a tree. Captain Ming did the same at the front.

"Away to your beds," he told Morag and Lucy. "Out at this hour of the day."

Morag yawned. Lucy kicked her shoes off, and fell asleep just as Captain Ming turned off all the puffer's lights, closing its eyes as well as Lucy's. She did not see the huge full moon low over the hills bring back something like day.

SIXTEEN

hen Lucy woke there was sunshine and early morning mist. Morag's eyes opened. She looked at Lucy.

"I lied," said Lucy, sorry for forgetting what loved Captain Ming, what he loved, and where he wanted to be. "To the mermaid."

"There was nothing there," said Morag.

Early morning birds called, small

things made the water talk; and there
was another gentle sound.

"Singing," said Lucy.

"I can't hear anything," said Morag.
She got out of her sleeping bag. Lucy
climbed out of hers and put her shoes
on. She found her comb, but her hair
was sticky with sea air and would take
too long to do. She dropped the comb,
got the bag with useful things in it, and
followed Morag out of the cabin.

Last night, after midnight, the puffer
had been tied fore and aft to moonlit
trees on a riverbank. Now there were no
trees. The engine was still, cold with
morning and dew. To right and left calm
water stretched off into mist. Captain
Ming laughed, some distance away, but
not on the puffer.

Below the stern was a circular
rocky island, rising a hand's breadth
from the water, with grass on it, rocks,

and small bushes. Beyond it was land with farms and fields, and a road with cars and wagons.

The rope ladder hung down to the island. Captain Ming sat there on a rock, gazing at something.

With her tail in the water, her elbows on land, the mermaid was talking or singing to him, or humming with her mouth open.

"We should wake Lachlan," said Morag.

"No," said Lucy. "He would sail away, and we would be in disgrace. We'll tell her it won't do."

"Tell him," said Morag. "He's only dreaming."

"I am dreaming too, if he is," said Lucy, "and about the exact same thing. If Captain Ming and I have both seen it then so have you, Morag."

"Exact same nothing," said Morag. "But . . ."

But, thought Lucy, means that you have seen what I've seen, life-size like the rest of the day.

"They're going to hold hands," she said.

"What will my mother say if we don't manage it?" said Morag. She went down the ladder first, and held it firm for Lucy.

The mermaid slapped the water with her tail, made faces at the newcomers, and rocked her head about.

"We ran on the land, after all," said Captain Ming cheerfully.

"She untied the ropes, the mischievous wee lassie, and brought us to her own island that we all thought was away beyond the bar and the river and indeed out to sea. But it's here we'll bide, her and me, on this crannog."

"I must be at the Academy each day," said Morag.

"Can the pair of ye not steer home up a wee river?" said Captain Ming. "I'll not be returning. This is my destiny, and I have foolishly forgotten it these last seven years."

The mermaid looked at Morag, and at Lucy. She sang Captain Ming a question.

"No," said Captain Ming, "these are not my lassies, and it isn't their way to grow tails."

The mermaid curled her tail round, to show it was more beautiful than legs, and stronger. She slapped the water, making a fountain and a wave, inviting people who were not Captain Ming to leave.

"Now, mermaid," said Morag, ignoring him, looking under the green hair into those seastorm eyes, "have you no husband under the sea to look after, and children of your own with tails?"

The mermaid stopped singing. She looked severely at Morag. Morag looked sternly back at her.

"Morag," said Captain Ming, "that is no way to be speaking to your new Auntie."

"And is your sister never to see you again?" said Lucy. "You will be in the sea, and on islands."

Morag was saying to the mermaid, "My mother does not think it right for you to take away her brother, when my granny is so ill. Though it's not that side of the family," she added truthfully. Captain Ming smiled at the mermaid. She smiled at him.

"You can't breathe water," Lucy said.

"That I will learn," said Captain Ming, impatiently. "It has happened before."

"She won't like you if you drown," said Lucy.

 The mermaid sat up in the water on her half-coiled tail, combing at her hair with her fingers.

"That's no good," Morag was saying to her. "I'll get you something." She went up the ladder, hurried along the deck, hurried back again, and down the ladder once more. She gave something to the mermaid.

"That's mine," said Lucy. "My unbreakable comb with Lyme Regis written on it."

"Her hair is so tangled," said Morag.

The mermaid touched the comb to her green hair.

"I wonder," said Captain Ming, rubbing his hands together, "whether Lachlan has enough fire to brew a mug of tea. Would she like one, do ye suppose?"

"Lachlan is asleep," said Morag. "You'd best get it yourself. And think how it will be without it."

"And if you did have it," said Lucy, "it would be made with salt water, every day."

The mermaid tugged the comb through green strands. "We'll help her while you get your tea," said Morag.

"I don't like to go," said Captain Ming. "It's seven years since I last saw her, and I'm full of every moment. But I would dearly like a last mug."

He stood up, not wanting to go, but wanting his tea. "You ken best, Morag," he said. "I want to be upriver and running the puffer, and she needs the sea, and there's no occupation for me on Faransay or Eanster. "Maybe," he went on, climbing the ladder, "we could take trips back and forth, I do not know."

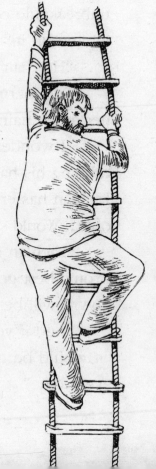

His voice could be heard, fading as it went into the engine room. There was a gush of smoke and a hiss of steam. The ship's boiler was waking up.

"Quarrelling already," said Morag. "Their first day. I hope it is their last and only one, also."

She helped the mermaid with the back of her hair. "It has sea things in it," she said, shaking the comb. The mermaid picked up a tiny brown crab as it scuttled away, and ate it like a toffee.

"When you go," said Lucy to her, "keep the comb."

The mermaid looked at the comb, at her smooth hair, and blinked. It was not enough for a parting gift.

"We have to think," said Lucy. Her eyes saw the fields beyond the island, and cars on the road. A car had stopped on the road. People were getting out, their faces towards the puffer. "The mermaid is only here for Captain Ming, and that's what matters."

The mermaid ran the comb through the green hair, after each stroke popping things into her mouth. Mermaids might be magical and rare, yet greedy for disgusting morsels too.

"Lucy," said a voice. It was not the voice of the mermaid, or of Morag, Captain Ming or Lachlan; nor was the speaker at all glad to have seen her.

SEVENTEEN

Lucy," said Craig, of all people, running across the edge of the field and on to the mermaid's island.

"Craig," said Lucy. "How awful."

"We just stopped the car," said Craig, "to look at the boat. I didn't want to see you."

"Craig," said Lucy, laying aside important matters, "this isn't Ashton in Cornwall."

"Big mistake, eh?" said Craig.

"We don't need you," said Lucy, bravely.

"I saw you in Glasgow, and somewhere else before," said Craig.

"We don't need you," said Lucy. "We're busy."

"We're talking to a mermaid," said Morag. "Unfortunately. I remember you. You were awful."

"It's how I get by," said Craig.

"He was really useful with Kelpie," said Lucy. "He really was, or you would have lost Kelpie."

Morag looked undecided. "Weel," she said.

"She doesn't believe in Kelpie," Lucy told Craig. "But she's glad to have him back."

"For the tourists only," said Morag.

"You have to know what you're doing," said Craig.

Craig looked at her, at Morag, and

at the mermaid. He sat on the rock
where Captain Ming had been sitting.
"I've seen some of those," he said. "In
the sea. We did a cruise. What is it?"

"It's a mermaid," said Morag.

"I'll buy it," said Craig. "We've got
a pond."

Someone on land shouted for Craig.
He took no notice. "You have to know
what to do with animals," he said to
Lucy. "They are all handicapped, the
way aliens think humans are."

Lachlan looked down from the puffer. "I've steam up," he said. "Himself is safe on board and we can be away in a minute. Up ye come or be left behind."

The mermaid still looked up at the puffer, expecting Captain Ming. She wants to be in the sea, thought Lucy, but not without Captain Ming.

"Don't let him come," she called to Lachlan.

"There is nothing I can do," said Lachlan. "He is getting his pack of gear and, Oh my Good Lord, no Captain, not that."

"What?" Morag called. But they knew at once.

They heard Captain Ming on the deck, out of sight, blowing up the bag of his pipes, with the drones buzzing.

He stood at the stern, the bag under his arm, the chanter in his hand, the blow pipe to his lips, and, looking at the horizon, he started a skirl.

Craig looked startled. Morag said, "He has no idea." Lucy covered her ears. Lachlan vanished into his engine room.

The mermaid fell down in the water, troubled and tearful. She thought she was being shouted at. She grabbed at Craig's hand. He had to bend to hold it.

"Lucy," he called, "She wants to be in the sea. You can help again, like with the water-horse. Which way is it?"

"Follow the run of the water," Lachlan called, above the noise of the pipes.

"*Lucy*," said Craig. It was an order.

"He's like that," said Lucy. "Has to have it all his own way. If I help will Captain Ming hate me?"

"Get her where she belongs," said Morag.

"Follow the shore round the sandbar," Lachlan called. "It is the salt water beyond."

Craig was knee-deep in the river now. The mermaid slapped the water with her tail, going along with him, getting angry, beginning a harsh song.

"It's cold, and that dirndum will deafen me," Craig called. "She's splashing like a demon, and these are my holiday clothes."

The splashing stopped when the mermaid reached deeper water. She lay still on her face, her hair streaming alongside her.

"Get hold," said Craig, wading out waist-deep and trying to lift her. "She has to breathe," he said. "Get in the water, stupid." He meant Lucy.

The water was colder than Lucy expected. When it reached her waist her breath died in her throat. Morag followed her. Her teeth rattled. "We should have life-jackets," she said. "This is too deep to paddle."

"Lift it up," said Craig. "And get walking."

Captain Ming was still showing off his skill with the pipes.

Lucy saw the rising tide on the sandbar, the sea lifting over the river. Colder water bit her chest.

The mermaid tasted salt and twitched her tail. She gurgled a fragment of song. She swung her hair.

"She's right, now," said Craig. "She's off."

She was not off just yet. She hung in the salt water, splashing it over herself. There were no more tears, but there was not quite a smile.

"Give her something," said Craig.

"She's got my comb," said Lucy.

"In your bag," said Craig. "Show her, Lucy."

The mermaid seemed not to see the swimming badge no mermaid would need. She chose the snowman's eyes, taped up like a small grey stone, lying on Lucy's palm.

"She's seen stones before," said Craig,

scornfully. He was standing on a beach
of them.

The tape grew wet, and fell away.
The snowman's eyes cracked open and
looked at the sky. The golden ammonite
shone bright in the morning sun.

Captain Ming started another tune,
got lost, started again, and ran out of
breath; the pipes groaned.

The mermaid lifted herself from the water. She stretched out her hand and took the golden ammonite in both hands, and swam with strokes of her tail over the sandbar in the swell. As she went she sang, raising her hands to show the glittering thing.

Lucy's toes had lost their senses, and her hands could neither feel nor be felt. She was like the findings bag, wet, cold, and empty. She turned to the puffer.

Craig went across the land in a different direction, towards people who were shouting for him.

"Fancy wanting him," said Lucy. But she felt sorry for Craig because he could manage strange animals but not enjoy the strangeness.

"Wave," said Morag, pulling Lucy along.

Craig looked back towards them, then turned away, not taking any notice. He's like that, Lucy thought. He doesn't care about real people.

Someone else waved, and called. The mermaid was pillowed on the gentle estuary waves, singing, splashing with her tail, and combing her hair. She laid herself back under a quilt of foam.

"It's done," said Morag.

By the road Craig was hustled into his own car, and the doors were banged shut very firmly.

"It'll be a job coming down," Captain Ming was saying, wondering how to manage the rope ladder with mugs of tea. "And Lachlan impatient to be off."

"We'll come up," said Morag.

Captain Ming helped them off the top of the ladder. Three mugs of tea were on the deck. "I didn't bring her one," he said. "I see she's gone."

"That's it," said Morag.

Captain Ming sipped at his tea. "Losh, excuse my language," he said, "this is hot." Certainly something brought tears to his eyes for a moment,

and he wiped his nose with one of Lachlan's oily rags. "We'll get upriver, if one of you will sound the whistle to wake Lachlan. Ye'd best sit by the engine and help Lachlan make porridge to set us right."

Only Morag is sensible, thought Lucy. Captain Ming and I both want to have a cry, but we can't.

Morag took her to the cabin to change into the Glasgow kilts before the porridge.

The mermaid girl, Kathryn, at the village by the flowery loch, tied the puffer up again. This time a boat came to meet them.

"It's my mother," said Morag. "Come to meet us, and bringing our dinners."

"It's mine too," said Lucy. "Mum, you'll have to climb the rope ladder, and it's very difficult the first time." And just to encourage her she ran up to the bridge and blew the whistle three times.

On deck Mrs MacAlister took a good look at her brother.

"You had no trouble with the mermaid, then?" asked Mum. "I've heard a lot about her."

"Mermaid?" said Morag. "What's that?"

"But," said Lucy, "you talked to her, and you gave her my comb."

"Talked to her, indeed?" said Morag.

"I only said what I would have said if
she had been there, but that didn't mean
she was. Imaginary things can't be there."

———

"It went back where it belonged," said
Craig, after the holidays. "The sea is full
of them. They just take looking at, and
then you see them."

"I saw her without that," said Lucy.
"Magical."

"You know nothing about looking,"
said Craig. "Or magical and that. It's just
what's there, so there's no fuss to be
made."

He handed Lucy a small package.
Inside it was a small dry crab. "It was in
my pocket," he said. "It's been washed."

"Thank you, Craig," said Lucy. "You
are very thoughtful."

"Get out," said Craig.

But he has already closed the door, thought Lucy. So I can't.

Somewhere on the tide, near Faransay or Eanster or Clowder, is a golden ammonite from Lyme Regis, part of a mermaid's treasure. But there, thought Lucy, everything is for something, if it can find it.